Top Cat

Lois Ehlert

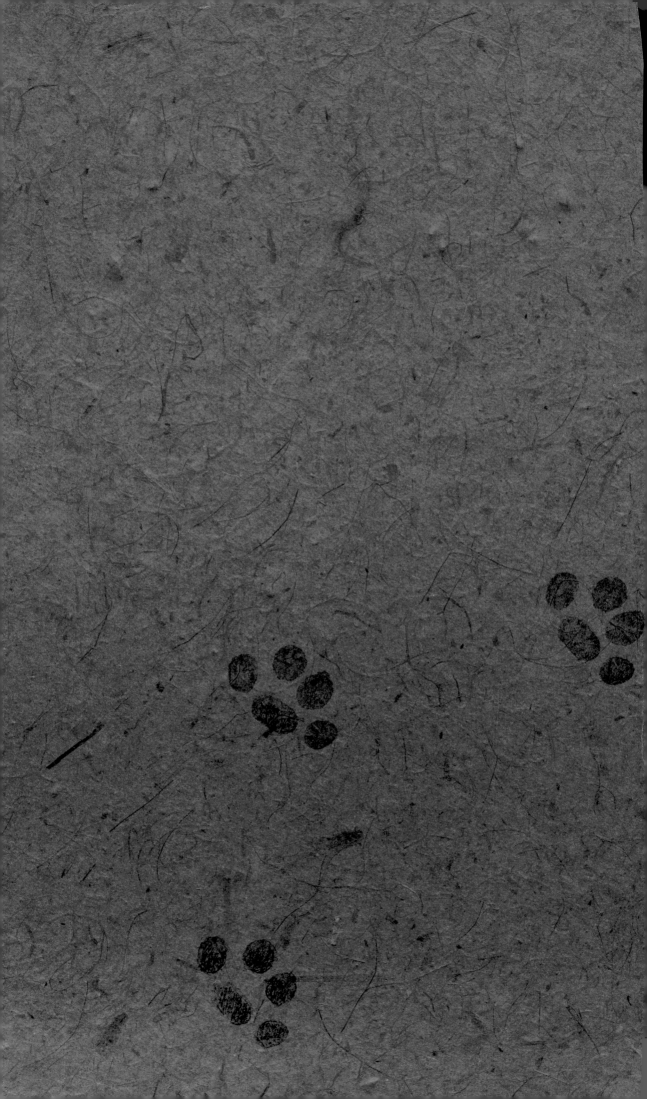

Top Cat

SCRITCH
SCRATCH

Lois Ehlert

SCHOLASTIC INC.
New York Toronto London Auckland Sydney
Mexico City New Delhi Hong Kong

O-KA-LEE
O-KA-LEE

I'm top cat.
Pet me, I'll purr.

I guard this place
in my coat of fur.

PURR
URR
PURR
URR

Boring job! Never see a
Nothing much happens
in this dull house.

mouse.

CREEEK
SLAM

THUMP

SCRATCH
SCRATCH

Who let you in?
One cat's
enough.

ME-OW
SCRATCH
SCRATCH
SCRATCH
ME-OW

SNIFF
SNIFF

I don't want to
share my stuff.

HMAN
CIETY

SWISH
SWISH

SWISH
SWISH

Go away, cat!

GRRRR
HISS
HISS

You've
invaded
my space.

SWISH
SWISH

CHEEP
CHEEP
CHEEP

GRRRR
HISS
HISS

And I don't like your cute little face.

SWISH
SWISH

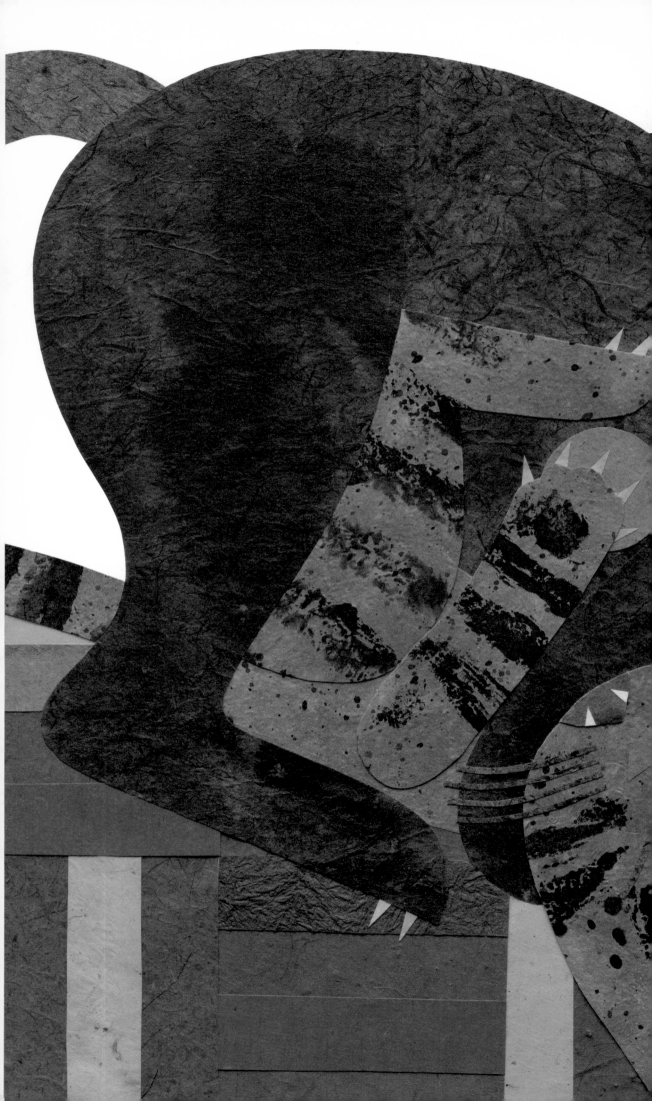

I'll fight you and bite
you behind the ear.
Get the message?
I'm boss
around here.

Well, you're here
to stay.
I can see that.

SCRATCH
SCRATCH

Guess I'm
stuck with you,
striped cat.

SWISH

JINGLE
JINGLE

THUNK

But
there's
more to do
than eat
and sleep.

JINGLE
JINGLE

WHIZ

Keep your
green eyes
open.
Watch me
leap!

Bounce on the couch. Leave lots of hair.

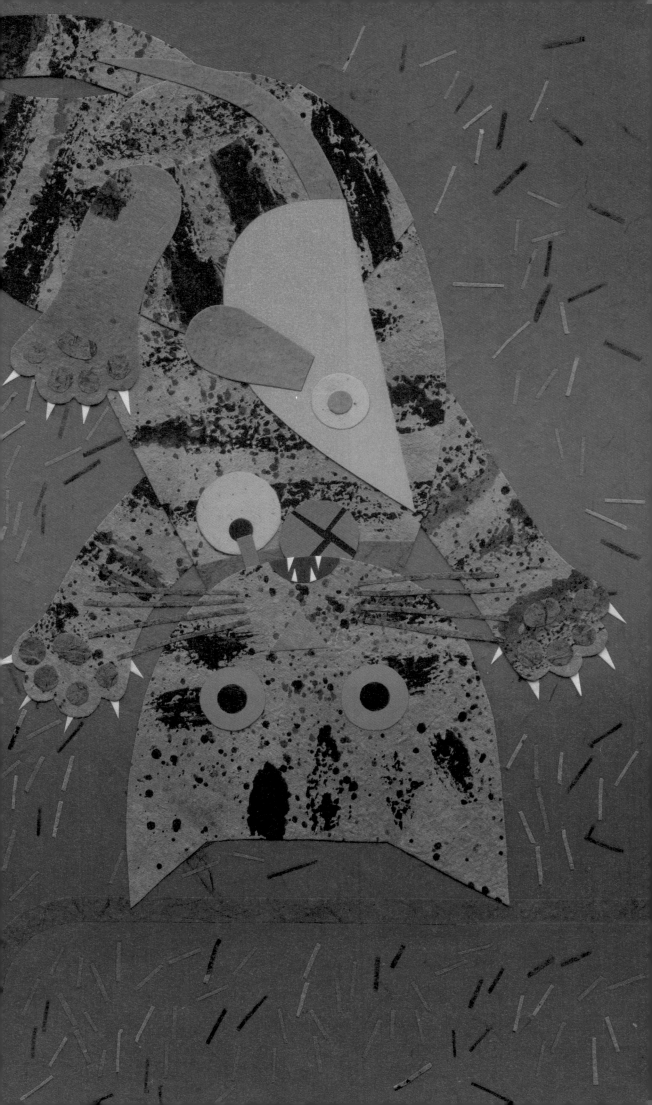

Eat leaves till
the plants are bare.

CHOMP

CHOMP

Drink from the sink when

DRIP

ompany's there.

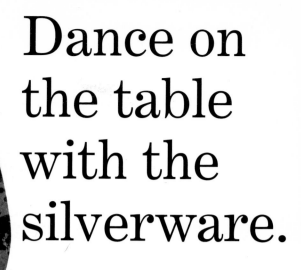

Dance on
the table
with the
silverware.

JINGLE
JINGLE

CLINK
CLANK

Door's
left open?
Go get
some
fresh air.

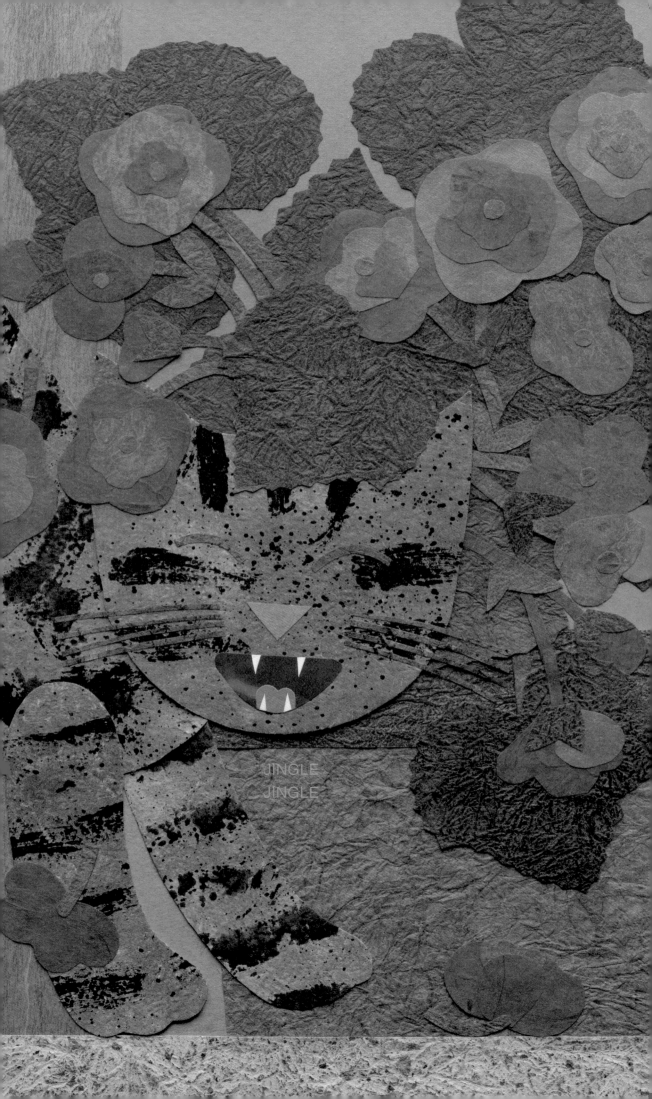

Test your claws.
Give birds a good scare.

FLAP
FLAP

O-KA-LEE
O-KA-LEE
O-KA-LEE

FLIT
FLIT

JAY
JAY
JAY

CHIRP
CHEEP

JINGLE
JINGLE

Time
to eat!
You'd
better
decide.

Will you come in
or stay outside?

WHAT
CHEER
WIT
WIT
WIT

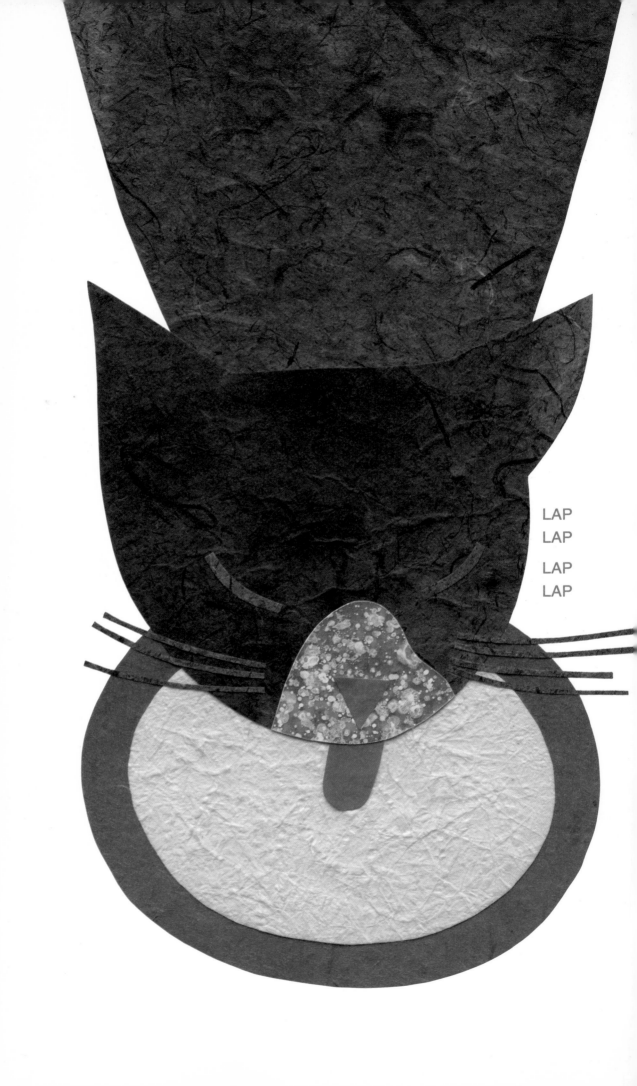

LAP
LAP
LAP
LAP

Welcome back!
Let's drink milk
in our furs.
No hisses,
no scratches,
no bites.

Just
purrs.

LIP
LIP
LIP
LIP

For Shirley and Don

ISBN 0-439-13738-1

Copyright © 1998 by Lois Ehlert.
All rights reserved.
Published by Scholastic Inc., 555 Broadway,
New York, NY 10012, by arrangement with
Harcourt Brace & Company.
SCHOLASTIC and associated logos are trademarks and/or
registered trademarks of Scholastic Inc.

12 11 10 9 8 7 6 5 4 3 2 1   9/9 0 1 2 3 4/0

Printed in the U.S.A.   08

First Scholastic printing, September 1999

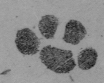